This book
belongs to:

_____

_____

EGMONT

We bring stories to life

First published in Great Britain 2006
by Egmont UK Limited
239 Kensington High Street, London W8 6SA
BARBIE and associated trademarks and trade dress are owned by,
and used under license from, Mattel, Inc.
© 2006, Mattel, Inc.

ISBN 1 4052 2699 4
ISBN 978 1 4052 2699 8

1 3 5 7 9 10 8 6 4 2

Printed in China

Based on the original screenplay by Cliff Ruby and Elana Lesser

Special Thanks to Vicki Jaeger, Monica Okazaki, Rob Hudnut, Shelley
Dvi-Vardhana, Jescya C. Durchin, Shea Wageman, Jennifer Twiner McCarron,
Greg Richardson, Vera Zivny, Rene Toye, Lil Reichman, Sean Newton,
Kevin Chai, Derek Toye, Pam Prostarr, Sheila Turner, and Walter P. Martishius.

Once upon a time, in a not too distant land, lived the wise King Randolph. The king had twelve beautiful daughters who loved to dance and sing and play. Sadly, the queen, the girls' mother, had died. Yet, the princesses were happy girls who loved their father very much.

But as time passed the king began to think that his daughters were not growing up as young princesses should. He wondered why they were never invited to balls in neighbouring kingdoms, or why no princes came to call at the palace. He decided to ask his cousin, the Duchess Rowena, to come to the palace and help him care for the princesses.

The king began to tell his daughters about his plans at lunch the next day.

"Girls, I have been thinking…" began the king. But he didn't get any further. The butler had announced the arrival of the royal cobbler and the girls were rushing to the garden to see their new dancing shoes, forgetting in an instant that their father had been talking.

The princesses gathered eagerly around the young cobbler, Derek, and his colourful talking bird, Felix.

Derek began handing out beautiful pairs of shoes. Each pair was a different colour specially chosen for each princess.

"Do you have anything for me?" asked Genevieve, quietly.

Turning shyly to her, Derek handed Genevieve the most beautiful pair of shoes the princess had ever seen.

"Wow!" gasped Genevieve.

"Come on, Genevieve," called Hadley, one of the twins. "Let's dance!"

The young cobbler watched the dancing princesses and let out a deep sigh. "I will never be able to dance with Princess Genevieve, Felix. I am just a cobbler and she is a princess!"

"Wait and see," squawked the bird. "Wait and see!"

The next week the princesses were summoned to the great hall to greet their cousin, Duchess Rowena.

"Welcome, Rowena," called the king. "Come and meet my daughters. May I present – Ashlyn, Blair, Courtney, Delia, Edeline, Fallon, Genevieve, Hadley, Isla, and the triplets Janessa, Kathleen and Lacey."

Rowena took a long walk up and down the line of smiling girls.

"Well I can see we have a lot of work to do," she said, sternly. "But I don't suppose it will take me long to make proper princesses out of them."

Twelve pairs of eyes turned to their father, wondering what was going on. The old king blushed. "I tried to tell you all, but you were just too busy to listen. Duchess Rowena is going to be in charge of your upbringing now. She will teach you to behave like proper princesses!"

Rowena was very quick to take control of palace life. She banned the girls from singing and dancing, made them wear horrible grey dresses that all looked alike, and punished them if they didn't do as she said.

One day, Genevieve went to talk to her father. "Papa," she said hesitantly. "It's about cousin Rowena. She keeps changing everything. Can't we go back to how we were, please?"

The king smiled at Genevieve. "Now, now," he said. "Rowena only wants what is best for you. She is staying!"

Very soon, King Randolph fell ill. The doctor came and looked at him, but as the days and weeks passed he continued to grow weaker.

Rowena stayed very close to the king's side, giving him cup after cup of soothing tea, but nothing seemed to make him any better.

A sadness seemed to fall over the palace, as the princesses were only able to see their father for brief moments each day. They saw more and more of the wicked Rowena who watched everything they did very closely.

On the evening of the triplets' fifth birthday, the princesses were sitting in their bedroom. Rowena had banned the girls from celebrating.

"Don't worry," Genevieve told the triplets. "We made sure Rowena didn't know about these!" And she handed the youngest girls a book each. It was the tale of *The Twelve Dancing Princesses*. The queen had left all her daughters a copy of the book to be given to them on their fifth birthdays. Each book had a different flower drawn on the front.

"Do you remember what happens to the princesses?" asked Genevieve.

"They find a magic gateway into a land where they can dance all night!" replied Lacey.

As Genevieve looked at Lacey's book she noticed that the flower on the cover exactly matched a flower carved into a stone on the bedroom floor. In fact the flowers on all the girls' books matched flowers carved into the floor.

And so, just like princesses in the book, Genevieve began to dance across the stones. On the last one she twirled three times. As she finished her last twirl the floor below her began to open and a bright light shone from below!

"This must be the way to the enchanted kingdom from the story," thought Genevieve.

And grabbing her kitten, Twyla, she began walking down the stairs to the magic gateway, below…

Passing through the gateway, Genevieve emerged at the edge of an enchanted lake. Across the lake sat an island with a beautiful pavilion, covered in flowers made from rubies, diamonds and emeralds.

Genevieve's sisters had been quick to follow her through the gateway and now they all climbed into a boat and crossed to the island. As they sailed, their nightgowns changed from their ordinary dull colour to bright, shimmering balldresses.

"Wow," gasped Lacey. "It's just perfect for dancing." No sooner had she said this than the flowers bent their heads and released a glistening cloud of magic dust. Notes of music began to swirl around the girls who leapt to their feet and danced.

"Ouch!" cried Lacey, suddenly. She had fallen whilst trying to copy her sisters' graceful dancing.

"Let's go and wash it," said Genevieve, taking her down to the edge of the lake. Genevieve gently bathed Lacey's knee. As soon as the water touched her knee the cut healed – instantly!

The princesses gasped in amazement, then rushed off to re-join the fun!

The next day all twelve girls were very tired at breakfast. Courtney even managed to fall asleep in her porridge!

Rowena looked at them suspiciously, wondering what they had been up to all night.

"Desmond," she called to her manservant. "Keep an eye on those girls tonight. Make sure no one comes or goes from their room."

"There is a Mr Fabian to see you, Duchess," announced the butler. Rowena blushed and rushed off to receive her guest.

As Genevieve was trying to rouse her sisters she glanced out of the window and noticed Rowena handing a package to the strange-looking Mr Fabian.

"Whoever can he be?" wondered Genevieve.

Later the same day the princesses took their shoes to the young
cobbler to get them repaired.

"Is that gold dust?" asked Derek, looking at Genevieve's shoes.

Genevieve giggled "We've been dancing," she replied. Twirling
around the puzzled cobbler. "One, two, three… four, five, six…
seven, eight, nine… ten, eleven, twelve… and twirl three times."

Derek looked on, dazzled by Genevieve's wonderful dancing.
As the princess came to a stop she had an idea.

"Derek?" she asked. "Do you know a man named Mr Fabian? Earlier I saw Rowena give him something. Could you find out who he is?"

"Of course, your highness," agreed the cobbler, feeling very special.

That night, Rowena's servant stood outside the princesses' bedroom all night. Nobody came or went through the door, but the princesses didn't stay in their room. They returned to the enchanted kingdom where once again they danced till their shoes were worn through.

The next day the Duchess stormed into the princesses' bedroom.

"Let me see your dancing shoes," she demanded. "These are worn through and they were new yesterday. I want an explanation!"

The princesses couldn't lie. First one then the other told the story of the enchanted kingdom. But Rowena wouldn't believe them and thought they were lying to her. To punish them she made them clean the front garden and the stone steps.

That night Rowena asked the princesses to tell her again where they had really been the night before.

"But we really were in the magical kingdom!" they all cried.

Rowena was furious and locked the girls in their bedroom. The poor princesses felt totally miserable and wished the horrible duchess had never come to the palace. Although they didn't want to leave their father they decided to run away to the enchanted kingdom forever!

Sadly, Genevieve began her dance across the flower-covered stones. "One, two, three…"

While the princesses were getting ready to travel to the enchanted kingdom, Derek had found the mysterious Mr Fabian, who admitted that he was selling Rowena strange potions.

Derek went straight to the palace to tell the princesses. But he found their room empty. They had already gone! Climbing into their bedroom, he noticed the stone flowers carved into the floor. He remembered Genevieve's strange dance in the garden and began to copy it...

But Rowena had seen Derek. She followed him into the enchanted kingdom. Quickly, she stole some of the magic flowers then rushed back to the palace. Ordering Desmond to smash the floor covering the gateway, she closed the entrance to the enchanted kingdom forever!

Meanwhile, Derek had told the princesses what he knew about Rowena and Mr Fabian. When they heard his story, the princesses desperately wanted to return to their father. Finding the entrance blocked, Genevieve looked around and spotted the magic flowers.

"I wish for another way out of the enchanted kingdom," she whispered.

No sooner had she wished it, than more dancing stones appeared. Genevieve and the handsome cobbler stepped lightly across the stones and the rest of the princesses followed them through the magic gateway and back into the palace gardens.

The girls emerged from the enchanted kingdom to find that Rowena had made herself queen and hired a new set of guards to protect her.

By working together the sisters were able to distract the guards, allowing Genevieve and Derek to slip inside the palace.

But it was too late. Rowena had already given King Randolph the last of the potion and he lay limp on the bed.

Just then, Rowena noticed Genevieve. Producing magic flower dust from her pocket, the duchess wished for armour to protect her. Suddenly, suits of armour around the room came to life and began to advance on Derek and Genevieve!

Outside the palace the triplets were hiding in a bush waiting for their sisters to return.

Lacey pulled a small bottle of water from around her neck. "I have to give Papa this," she said. "It's from the magic lake; it might be able to help him!" And she ran off to the palace.

Her short little legs carried her as fast as they could. But they were no match for the giant Desmond who was waiting at the bottom of the stairs. He scooped her up and carried her to the king's bedroom.

"Lacey," gasped Genevieve. Derek and Genevieve stopped fighting immediately.

"Now I will be queen," cackled Rowena. "And because you love dancing so much you can dance for the rest of your lives!"

Rowena took a magic flower from her pocket and blew some dust towards Genevieve and Derek.

Genevieve pulled her fan from her dress and waved it at the magic dust. It blew the dust right back at Desmond and Rowena, who began to dance around the room!

Genevieve and Derek held their breath as the evil duchess and her mean butler danced and danced, all the way into the great hall and out of the palace. They watched in amazement as they danced off into the distance, knowing they would never return…

The king, however, was still in danger. Lacey quickly climbed onto the bed beside her father and opened the little bottle. As Lacey poured a few drops onto her father's lips he began to wake up.

"Lacey...Genevieve," said the king, opening his eyes. "I am sorry. Rowena was poisoning me and I didn't even notice. She was so horrible to you. Will you ever forgive me?"

"Of course, Father," cried Genevieve throwing her arms around him. "We are so happy that you are well again!"

Not long after that the king gave his blessing to Derek and Genevieve and they were married in a beautiful ceremony.

"See," squawked Felix. "Who says a cobbler can't dance with a princess!"

"Miaow," agreed Twyla.

The princesses cheered and clapped and began to dance through the great hall. In the middle of them all danced Derek and Genevieve looking as happy as could be.